# Unholy Womb

## and other Halloween Tales

### Steven E. Wedel

This is a work of fiction. Any resemblance to real people, living or dead is purely coincidental or used fictitiously.

No part of this work may be reproduced in whole or part without the express written permission of the author.

MoonHowler Press

MoonHowler Press, Oklahoma, USA

# DEDICATION

This collection is dedicated to everyone who turns on their porchlight on October 31 to offer treats to the little tricksters. Keep the tradition alive.

# Contents

# Unholy Womb

The horror began on a day Danny believed to be a perfect prelude to autumn. Autumn was his favorite season; the air was charged with electricity, harvest smells filled the breezes and gave the first winter goose pimples. But most of all, the season led to The Day.

Halloween.

It was because of the coming holiday that Danny was walking along the sidewalk of Ash Street in his little town of Windfall, Illinois. A breeze sent leaves scurrying around his feet with a sound like old bones knocking together. Danny was going to get a pumpkin for his Halloween jack-o-lantern. For as long as he could remember, he had been getting pumpkins from Farmer Sutton.

Of all the farmers who grew pumpkins around Windfall, Farmer Sutton was Danny's favorite. They had an agreement through an old friendship between the farmer and Danny's father; Danny got the privilege of going through the entire pumpkin patch before the majority was trucked off to market and the rest picked over by the townspeople that came to Sutton's farm for their jack-o-lanterns.

Danny didn't think he would have any trouble securing two pumpkins from his friend this year.

The sidewalk he was traveling on showed cracks and was crumbling in places as he neared the edge of town. The walk soon petered out completely and Ash Street changed from a paved avenue to a dirt road. Danny kept walking. He had forgotten about the rundown little shack he had to pass on his way out of town – until he looked up and saw the ramshackle building where Voodoo Charlie lived. He hurried to the other side of the road.

The dwelling was gray from lack of paint and only about as large as Danny's father's tool shed. Bowed two-by-fours held a sagging roof over a packed-dirt porch. The shingles remaining on the building were of rotted pine; a rusty stovepipe pointed crookedly at the sky.

As he crept past, a little white dog left his place in front of the door and ran under the fence and across the road to bark at Danny's heels. Danny knew from previous journeys that the dog wouldn't bite him, so his only worry was that the noise the little cur made would bring his owner from the shack. But Voodoo Charlie didn't come out of the house.

Danny made two more turns and then the Suttons' farm came into view, acres of gold, with small splotches of just-ripening pumpkins under the waving corn stalks. A quarter of a mile up the dirt road was the driveway that led to the pale green farmhouse.

Coming from the direction of the drive, and less than half that distance away, was a shuffling scarecrow. Danny's heart increased its pace as he realized he would have to confront Voodoo Charlie after all. For the second time, Danny crossed the road to be as far away as possible from the old man.

As Danny crossed the road, Voodoo Charlie stopped walking. He stood on his side of the dirt lane and watched the boy advance.

The closer Danny came to the waiting figure, the more features he recognized: the stained tan pants, the yellow shirt with black buttons and a limp collar, the dusty brown shoes, and dark, withered skin of the hands and wrists. Voodoo Charlie's short gray hair curled close to his scalp. There were bags under his eyes and deep lines marked his chocolate-brown face like cracks on a dirty egg. As Danny passed, he could see the few remaining teeth in Voodoo Charlie's mouth, rotted black and yellow. A pink tongue licked the gaping, crooked holes.

"Goin' ta git yer Hallereen punkin?" Voodoo Charlie asked in his cracked voice.

Danny tried to answer, but only managed to croak a positive response. He didn't stop walking.

"Git a biggun," the ancient black man said as Danny passed.

Danny upped his brisk pace until he turned onto the dirt driveway leading to the little farmhouse. Heck, the Sutton's golden retriever, greeted him halfway up the drive. Mrs. Sutton appeared on the porch of the house and a smile spread over her plump, farmwife face.

"Hi, Mrs. Sutton," Danny said, hopping onto the porch beside the woman.

"Hello, Danny," she answered. "Come on in. I just took an apple pie out of the oven a little while ago. I don't think Gene's ate it all yet." She turned to lead him into the house. The dog followed behind Danny, tail wagging as if he, too, wanted a piece of pie. "No, Heck, you can't come in. Go on." Mrs. Sutton shooed the dog off the porch. He began to chase one of the chickens that had wandered to the front of the house. Mrs. Sutton shook her head at the dog's antics. "Spoiled rotten," she whispered to Danny.

Inside the kitchen, they found Farmer Sutton sitting at the table eating a piece of steaming pie. He had obviously just come in from the fields; dust coated his faded bib overalls and red flannel shirt, the sleeves of which were rolled up past his elbows. His blue eyes lit up and his whiskery face split into a grin when he saw Danny.

"Hi there, boy," he boomed. "The old lady there was just telling me today that you'd probably be over soon. For once, she was right." He winked at Danny.

Mrs. Sutton, who had gone to a cupboard to get a plate for Danny's pie, turned at the remark – she too was smiling. "Watch what you say, old man. I just might take a rolling pin to your head."

Danny noticed the huge pumpkin on the countertop near the sink. It was two pumpkins, actually, Siamese twins grown together to form one vegetable. They had grown together at an angle so that when one sat directly upright, the other was tilted. The odd gourd was still green on much of its surface.

"Do you like it?" Farmer Sutton asked.

Danny nodded, his mouth full of pie.

"We thought we'd carve two faces in it, like on Truth or Consequences, one happy, one sad. What do you think?"

"That'll look good," Danny replied, thinking it would be a good time to make his request for an extra pumpkin. Mrs. Sutton spoke before he could.

"I guess I'll go out and finish hanging up the laundry now that Gene got rid of that nutty black man."

Danny tried hard to swallow a mouthful of pie, but by the time he got it down, Mrs. Sutton had already gone out the back door. "Voodoo Charlie was here?" he asked the farmer.

"Yes, he was here. Again, I should say." Gene Sutton shook his head. "I don't know what it is about that old man. We haven't bothered him, but he's been hanging around a lot lately. I've lost count of the times I've caught him in the fields. He started coming around just after I fertilized last winter, then he stopped until I started planting. Since then, he's been coming around every few weeks. I'll see him just meandering through the fields.

"It's not just here, either. All the other farmers I've talked to have told me he's been around their farms, too." He paused in his speech, then snorted. "I said we hadn't bothered him, that's true, but not completely. When I was a boy about your age I bothered him plenty – me and every other boy in town. Most of the girls, too. Do the kids still tease him?"

"Some," Danny said. "He doesn't come into town much." He paused, ate another bite of pie, then asked, "How old do you think he is?"

"I don't know. He looked exactly the same when I was a kid, and that was, well, a while back."

"Why does everyone call him Voodoo Charlie?"

"Because he's so weird, I guess. There used to be stories about him stealing dead babies from their graves to use in his evil potions." Farmer Sutton smiled, but immediately the man's laughter died and his face took on a troubled look. The past four or five years had seen a rash of grave robbing in the area, all the victims being infants.

The crimes had stopped just shortly before the previous winter.

"I better get back to work," Farmer Sutton said. "When you finish there you can just help yourself to the pumpkins. I'm sure you'll find one you like." He got up from his chair and turned toward the back door. His hand was turning the knob before Danny found the courage to speak.

"Mr. Sutton?" The farmer turned back to face him. "Would you mind if I took two pumpkins this year? There's this girl, and she asked me to carve one for her." Danny rushed the last words.

The farmer grinned broadly, winked, and said, "Sure, you take as many as you need."

Danny wolfed down the last few bites of apple pie and hurried to the pumpkin fields. It took him nearly two hours to find two pumpkins that would suit the faces he was planning to put on them. He carried them to the house and put them on the back porch. For the first time, he wondered how he would get them all the way home.

Mrs. Sutton provided the answer. "Think you can get them home in this?" She brought a rusty red wagon with squeaky wheels from the barn.

"Yes, thanks," Danny said, relieved to see the squeaking relic. He put the pumpkins in and took up the handle. "Well, thanks for the pumpkins. I better get home." The sun was already nearing the horizon and his shadow was long and dark. The air had taken on a nippy coolness.

"Okay, Danny. Have a nice Halloween."
"I will. You too."

Mrs. Sutton waited until Danny was nearly out of earshot before calling, "I hope your little girlfriend likes her pumpkin, too!"

Blushing from neck to hair, Danny only waved and hurried on up the drive. He could hear the woman laughing as she went inside the house.

Back on the road, he forced the blush off his face and concentrated on hurrying home.

He crossed to the other side of the road long before he reached Voodoo Charlie's shack. He hoped with every ounce of his being that he would not see the old black man. He willed the wheels of the wagon to be silent while he passed.

As soon as the ramshackle dwelling came into view, Danny saw the man in a rocking chair on the front porch. Voodoo Charlie rocked steadily and looked in the direction Danny came from, as if waiting on the boy.

The squeaking wheels brought the dog from his place at the old man's feet. He slipped under the fence and ran up the road, barking. The dog began his usual pouncing and nipping at Danny's heels. Danny saw the smile on Voodoo Charlie's face as he grew closer.

When Danny began to pass the house, the rocking chair ceased its motion. "Gotcha two ub'em, huh?" Voodoo Charlie asked.

"Yes." Danny never slowed his pace.

"Gude." The ancient black man grinned his rotted grin. "You have a gude Hallereen. You an all da utter kiddies. I know dat I sho will. Trick or treat!" he crowed, his voice cracking as he laughed hysterically. He slapped his skinny knees and rocked madly.

The rest of the journey home passed without problems. Danny took the vegetables to his room on the second floor and put them on his windowsill to finish ripening.

Two weeks later, on a Saturday, Danny's parents went to the grocery store for the week's shopping, leaving Danny home alone. The pumpkins were ripe enough for carving. Danny took a short butcher knife and went upstairs to cut out the hideous faces he had stored in his imagination.

He discovered Voodoo Charlie's trick almost too late.

Halfway across his room he detected movement from the direction of his window. He stopped and looked. His eyes widened as he saw a figure standing among the broken shards of one of the pumpkins.

The beast was just over eight inches tall and dull orange in color, like the rind of the pumpkin it had hatched from. It crouched on bowed legs, its potbelly tightening and relaxing as it breathed. Leathery wings tipped with small black horns rippled on its back. The hands and feet of the creature all ended in long, curved nails. Danny could see tiny muscles bulging on the small arms and legs. The orange head was about the size of a ping-pong ball, thick lips curled away from lethal yellow fangs. Pointed ears swept back from the side of the head; they twitched as the thing studied Danny. Two more black horns, slightly longer than those on the wings, protruded from the forehead in direct line with the bulbous, tan-colored eyes.

The bat-goblin let out a squeaky battle cry and hopped from the windowsill, its wings flapping. It came soaring through the room toward Danny's throat.

Danny did the only thing he could think of; he swung the knife as the creature drew close, stepping out of the way at the same time. The knife missed completely, but the step back kept the thing from getting his throat. The needle-sharp teeth sank into his arm instead.

Danny gasped in pain. The knife flew from his fingers. He tried to tear the monster off his arm by pulling on it just below its wings, but the teeth had a firm hold. The creature clawed at his flesh, leaving bloody scratches. Danny released the thing's torso and tugged sharply on one of the legs. The limb tore away from the body with a sound like raw meat on Styrofoam. Yellow goo trailed from the ragged end.

The creature's potbelly swelled with blood. Danny dropped the leg and went into a frenzy. He grabbed at the beast, pulling off the remaining limbs, the wings, and bits of the torso in gory handfuls that he dropped to the floor. Soon all that was left on his arm was the small, horned head, still sucking. Danny could feel the blood being drawn from his arm and watched as it drained out the ragged stump of the monster's throat.

Danny took the monster's head in his hand, squeezing while be pulled upward and away until it was dislodged from his arm. The fangs tore away small ribbons of flesh and the jaw began to snap loudly as it tried to get the teeth into Danny's fingers.

Danny dropped the head to the floor. The teeth continued to click together. He stomped on it with his sneakered foot. It made a sound like a chicken bone breaking. More yellow fluid oozed onto the carpet, mingling with the blood dripping from Danny's fingers.

*Voodoo Charlie did it! Voodoo Charlie did it!*

Danny rubbed his eyes, trying to clear his head. He could smell blood drying on his arm. He let his hands drop to his sides and his eyes found the window and the pumpkin that had not yet hatched. Danny stepped carefully over the pieces of his vanquished enemy and looked for the butcher knife.

He found it on the floor beside his bed. He took the knife to the window, gripping it tightly. He examined the pieces of the broken womb first, poking at them with the point of the knife before touching them with his fingers. The shards were dry and brittle, cracking and breaking into several more pieces at his touch. Danny noticed that there was none of the stringy pulp or small seeds that were supposed to be inside a pumpkin. He scraped the pieces to the floor and examined the other vegetable.

The orange skin still had several lighter patches on its rough surface. Cracks made dark veins on places where the pumpkin was completely ripe. Danny slid the point of the knife into the top of the orange globe a few inches from the stem and cut a circle. When the cut was complete, he withdrew his blade and lifted the top off the pumpkin.

The green stem continued on the inside of the vegetable, glistening moistly, unlike the dried stub on the outside. It coiled round and round to the small orange body lying in a fetal position on its back at the bottom of the pumpkin. The unborn monster was surrounded in a thin covering of orange pulp speckled with shriveled, tan seeds. The green umbilical cord went through the pulp and between the creature's knees to attach to its stomach.

The monster itself was not yet fully developed, but like the pumpkin's ripeness, its time was very close. The eyes were oversized, puss-filled bubbles, as were the tips of the fingers and toes where the claws would soon break through. The horns on its head were not yet as long as the previous creature's and looked much more delicate; the horns on the wing tips were the same. The thing did not move as Danny peered into the womb.

Danny wondered for a moment about what to do with the monster before he decided on the obvious conclusion. He pushed the point of his knife through the pulp and into the chest of the beast. Voodoo Charlie's creation did not even twitch as the knife sank home. The odor released from the body when the demon was aborted caused Danny to gag. He gave the knife a sharp jab, felt it pin the monster to the bottom of its womb, and then staggered back, the smell making him think of the "dead baby" jokes he had heard in school.

*What about the other pumpkins?*

Danny thought about the hundreds Farmer Sutton had grown, the thousands the other farmers around Windfall had raised and sent to market? Danny remembered Farmer Sutton telling him that the old Negro had been to all the farms around the town. Would people all over the country be getting a nasty trick courtesy of Voodoo Charlie this Halloween?

*What about the unusual pumpkin that had been sitting on the Sutton's kitchen counter?*

Danny left the house at a run, not bothering to wash the blood from his arm or even to leave his parents a note explaining where he had gone.

A cold wind blew in his face as he ran along the sidewalk of Ash Street. He pounded hundreds of multicolored leaves beneath his feet dodging an elderly man raking his front lawn and nearly colliding with a little girl on a tricycle. Soon the town dropped behind him. An extra burst of speed carried him past Voodoo Charlie's shack before the little white dog could even get under the fence to nip at his heels.

Danny turned the corner onto the road where Farmer Sutton lived and the little farmhouse sprang into view. Danny's run became a dead stop, and then a hurried but nervous walk when he saw the bent form of the ancient black man standing at the head of the Suttons' driveway.

Voodoo Charlie was watching the house. He seemed to be waiting on something. *Does he want to hear the screams of the farmer and his wife when their pumpkin hatches?*

Screams, Danny thought, that might be symbolic of the screams heard all over the nation. Danny forced himself to take the steps that brought him closer to the bent form of Voodoo Charlie.

He must have heard Danny's labored breathing and nervous steps approaching on the road. Voodoo Charlie turned to face him, and for a moment Danny thought sure the old man could taste his fear. The pink tongue licked the cracked lips through a hole where the teeth were missing. Voodoo Charlie smiled at him, and Danny looked away.

"Yer jest in time, boy," Voodoo Charlie said. "I think yer farmer friend is 'bout to have hisself a set o'twins." The old man began to cackle.

Danny sidled quickly past him and hurried up the drive. When the screams began, Danny started running toward the house. Behind him, Voodoo Charlie laughed harder.

Danny stepped onto the front lawn as Mrs. Sutton ran out of the house, her skirt flying around her knees. The screen door banged against the side of the house and then slammed closed. Heck bounded from the other side of the porch. Mrs. Sutton was screaming and waving her pudgy arms frantically. One of the orange pumpkin-monsters hung from her neck, its body swelling as it drained the blood from the woman. Heck saw the creature hanging from his mistress' neck and tried to jump high enough to tear it away, but Mrs. Sutton's movements prevented him from getting a hold on it. Over the woman's screams and the dog's barking Danny could still hear Voodoo Charlie cackling.

The monster burst. Danny was still several feet from the struggling group, but he was near enough to see the bloated body of the creature explode, and close enough to be sprayed by the flying goo. He wiped his face and hurried to where Mrs. Sutton had slumped to the ground.

Only the small orange head remained, still clinging to the woman's neck by its teeth, blood pumping from its throat. Heck was nosing at the head. Danny pushed the dog away and bent over Mrs. Sutton. He carefully pried the sucking head from her neck, but even as it came free he felt the strained pulse in the farmwife's throat flutter and die. Danny stomped the head to mush under his foot while tears leaked from his eyes. He hurried to the house, already sure what he would find.

From the living room, he could see the body of Farmer Sutton sprawled over the kitchen table, the broken pieces of the Siamese twin pumpkin scattered around him. The remains of his killer were splattered around the room; yellow specks, like mucus, clung to the walls and appliances. The head continued pumping a thin trickle of blood from the back of the farmer's neck onto the table, where it ran off and fell to the pool spreading across the linoleum floor.

Danny silently left the house.

It was quiet outside. The cold wind made the only sound. The golden retriever joined Danny on the porch of the farmhouse. Danny absently patted the dog's head and then went slowly down the steps, avoiding the corpse lying a few feet away, and started back up the drive.

The dog followed him a short way, then turned and went back. Danny let him go. Voodoo Charlie was nowhere in sight.

*What about the pumpkins? How long before reports start coming in of people attacked by little orange creatures that hatch from their Halloween jack-o-lanterns? What about Voodoo Charlie? Will he be caught and punished?*

At the edge of the driveway Danny found a crumpled heap of clothing: a yellow shirt with black buttons, a pair of almost-worn-out tan pants, and two dusty brown shoes. All that was left of Voodoo Charlie.

Almost.

A gust of October wind rocked Danny on his feet. As it blew past, he heard the dry, cackling laughter of the old black man and the hoarse words, "Happy Hallereen!"

# The Halloween Feast

The air in the car was growing chill. Lewis Robertson stopped the tapping noise he was making with the envelope on the steering wheel. Angrily, he tore the card from the envelope and re-read the words of the invitation.

On the front was a cartoonish picture of a ghoul. In the voice bubble above his head were the words, "Come to a Halloween party!" Inside was an address. Lewis checked for the hundredth time to be sure the address inside the invitation matched that of the building he was parked before; they were the same. He tossed the invitation to the passenger seat of his car.

He stared at the front of the building for a while longer. It was one of many abandoned warehouses along the waterfront, though not in as bad repair as most. Still, there were no other cars here and he had seen no sign of other people in the half-hour he had sat in front of the old building.

*Is it a joke?*

He hadn't wanted to come to any damn party anyway. He hadn't wanted to do anything for the past month except stay in his dark house and be left alone. He didn't need to work anymore; Beth's life insurance had paid the mortgage as well as all the other bills they had accumulated in their five years of marriage. And the policy they had taken out on little Brandon only two months before had been enough to pay the funeral expenses for both of Lewis's loved ones.

Lewis stopped that train of thought, afraid if he stayed on it he would begin crying again. He didn't want that; recently it had become too hard to stop the tears once they began. He thought instead of his mother and how she had nearly forced him to come to this nonexistent party.

"You haven't left the house in weeks," she had scolded. "This is a golden opportunity to get out and mingle with friends. You need that."

"How do I know this party is being given by any of my friends?" Lewis argued.

"Why else would you have been invited?" she countered. She had nagged until Lewis finally gave in and agreed to attend the party. He knew his mother was only concerned about him being shut up alone and brooding over the accident. She had made the red devil costume he was wearing.

"Shit!" he muttered as he suddenly threw open the car door and stepped out of the vehicle. "Might as well be sure it's just a damn joke." He slammed the door, then straightened his wiry tail behind him, pulled the red mask over his face and charged toward the door of the warehouse. A brisk wind brought the gooseflesh out beneath the thin material of his costume. From the other side of the warehouse, Lewis could hear the steady rhythm of the river slapping against the pilings. Thin fingers of fog drifted toward him, curled around his legs like lovers, and then broke apart to reform behind him.

*Knock? Or just go in, if the door is unlocked?* Lewis reached out and jerked on the door's handle. The wooden door opened with a groan of protest. Lewis quickly stepped inside and let the door close behind him. He was in an office. Another door faced him from the other side of the room. Lewis stepped to it and pulled it open as well. It led into the warehouse itself, and as it closed behind him, Lewis realized he was alone except for two tables in the center of the vast, dimly lighted storage area. He reached behind him for the door handle, ready to leave, angry at himself as well as his mother.

"Lewis, there you are." A hand came down on his shoulder and held him. The grip was cold and heavy. Lewis turned his head to face a tall, muscular man dressed as a Greek warrior. The man smiled, a twinkle in his eyes.

"Do I know you?" Lewis asked.

"Not yet," the man answered. "But we'll have a while to get to know one another."

"Am I the first to get here?" Lewis tried to grin.

"No, you're late. But you're the guest of honor, so it doesn't matter. As long as you're here."

"But I don't see anyone else," Lewis protested.

"Your eyes will adjust."

"Who are you?"

"Who do I look like?"

"I don't know," Lewis answered. "Hercules, or Achilles maybe."

"Odysseus, my friend. Odysseus."

"Okay, fine, but who are you really?"

"Does it matter?"

"I'd like to know."

"You'll know later, though by then I doubt you'll care about me."

"But – "

"Come, Lewis, let's have some punch." The man took him by the arm and led Lewis toward one of the two tables. Lewis could now see that there was a large punch bowl and a single glass on one table. The other was empty.

"One glass?" he questioned.

"Do you need more?" The man picked up the small glass and began stirring the sweet-smelling red punch with a ladle he held in the other hand.

"You miss your wife and child, don't you?" asked the man dressed as Odysseus.

"You know ..." Lewis eyed the man more suspiciously than before.

"We all know." Odysseus nodded. He filled the glass and handed it to Lewis.

Lewis lifted the glass and held it near his mouth, suddenly not sure he should drink. His host sensed his hesitation and laughed.

"It's not poisoned," he said. "Would you like for me to drink some, too?" He lifted the ladle and sipped from it, swallowing loudly.

Grinning sheepishly, but still unsure, Lewis took a small drink from the cup. He swallowed, and then noted the aftertaste, a thick, coppery, salty taste.

"There's blood in here!" He dropped the cup to the table, where it overturned and spread its contents in a shining puddle. "What the hell are you trying to – " Lewis choked on the words as he looked up from the spilled fluid.

"It is Halloween," he heard Odysseus say, but Lewis barely took notice of the words.

The warehouse was filled with people. They stood in bunches and talked amongst themselves, or flitted from group to group carrying news and gossip. Children scuttled among the adults, playing tag, laughing and shouting. Everyone kept glancing toward the table where he stood, Lewis realized, dumbfounded by what he was beholding.

"Your eyes have adjusted?" asked the voice of Odysseus.

"I – But – Where did they come from?"

"The Realm of Death, of course." There was a smile in the man's voice. "Here comes someone you will recognize."

Lewis turned, and his eyes widened as he saw Beth part from the crowd and move toward him, her arms outstretched. He ran to her and they embraced, her cold lips finding his and kissing him passionately.

"I missed you," Beth whispered.

"How can this happen?" Lewis asked, but before Beth could respond, the voice of Odysseus was ringing over the throng.

"Ladies and gentlemen," he called, "Our guest has arrived and tasted the drink we offered. Let the festivities begin." He clapped, and from somewhere came soft, urgent music.

Beth grasped his arms and began leading him in a dance Lewis did not recognize. All around them, other couples paired up and began moving with the rhythm of the music.

"I don't understand," Lewis whispered.

"You don't need to," Beth answered. "Just be with me, dance with me and love me."

Lewis pulled her closer and they danced to the unending music, tears of happiness running down his face.

Finally he was able to ask, "What about Brandon? Is he here?"

"Yes, he's playing with the other kids," Beth said. She looked around, and then pointed. "There he is."

Lewis followed her finger and found his four-year-old son tossing a ball to a girl of about the same age. Brandon's eyes met his, and Lewis saw his son mouth the familiar words, "Hi, Daddy." Then the child waved to him before returning to his game. There was a lump in Lewis's throat and he buried his face on the cold shoulder of his wife.

They danced again for what seemed only moments, but Lewis knew might actually be hours, before the music stopped and Beth put her lips to his ear.

"It's almost midnight. Halloween is almost over, and it's time for you to make a decision."

"Lewis!" Odysseus called from the center of the warehouse. "Come over here, and bring your lovely wife." Arm in arm, Lewis and Beth Robertson walked toward the tables.

The punch bowl and spilled glass remained on one table. The other table was still empty, but now Lewis saw that beneath it was another bowl, larger than the punch bowl, and empty.

"Lewis," Odysseus began speaking when the couple stood before him, "We are allowed to return to this world only one day every year. On that day, we must have sustenance, or the next year we may be too weak to return.

"Every year we must search among the living for one willing to help us," the man continued. "One who will feed us."

There arose a murmur from the assembled spirits.

"You have tasted the blood of all those who have gone before you, Lewis. The others who have helped us. It allowed you to see those you believed lost to you. Will you help us, and stay with us now, or will you return to the world of the living?"

"What – what is it you're asking me to do?" Lewis asked as he clutched Beth's arm tighter.

"Feed us from your living veins."

Another murmur from the crowd.

"Kill myself?"

"Yes, slay your body so that your soul may join us," Odysseus answered.

Lewis looked to Beth, and then down at the shadowy image of his son, Brandon, who had come to join them at the table. Brandon smiled up at him.

"It's for you to decide," Beth said quietly. Lewis turned back to her and looked intently into her large, soft eyes. "You can join us now, or wait until your natural time comes. You'll be with us again eventually. But, you need to decide now."

"Yes Lewis, we need your decision now," Odysseus concurred. The horde of spirits murmured once more. He motioned to the table and the bowl, and now Lewis saw a long, curved knife laying on the table. He knew he was supposed to put the glittering blade to his throat, let out the life, and join his family in this shadowy world of death. He reached for the knife.

The crowd shifted and Lewis could feel their excitement, their hunger for him. The knife was cold and heavy in his shaking hand.

"Lie on the table, with your head off the edge so the bowl can catch your offering," Odysseus instructed.

Lewis stepped closer to the table and then stopped. A shudder ran down his body as he considered what he was ready to do. *Suicide.* Slice his own throat open with this razor-sharp blade. His eyes shifted to find Beth and Brandon; their faces were impassive and their thoughts unreadable. He would join them, Lewis thought, just as Beth had said, if not now, eventually.

"I can't," he whispered as he dropped the knife to the table. The spirits became angry, frustrated. He felt something cold being slipped into his right hand, and then his left arm was taken in an equally chill grip. Beth was holding his arm and Brandon had come to hold his father's hand. Lewis felt the warm tears running down his face.

"We'll wait, Daddy," Brandon promised.

"Yes, we have nowhere to go." Beth smiled at him. Lewis nodded. No words would come through his throat.

"But you have somewhere to go, Lewis." The voice of Odysseus was stern and angry. "You must leave here immediately. Go."

"Good-bye," Beth whispered. She was fading from his sight as Lewis watched. He reached for her, trying to hold her to him, but she was like a wisp of steam that slipped through his desperate fingers.

"Bye Daddy." Brandon was already gone, leaving only a cool place in the palm of his father's hand.

Lewis turned and ran from the warehouse as the other ghosts faded. He ignored their curses as well as their pleas. He fumbled for his keys as he ran, and then he was in the car and driving, not caring where he went or what route he took.

He drove for hours, and eventually found himself parked on a narrow gravel road that ran beside the river a few miles outside the city limits. It was a favorite spot for fishing. He had brought Beth and Brandon here many times for picnics beside the water. Brandon had caught his first fish, a small, slimy catfish, from this place.

"I should have done it," Lewis said to himself. "I'm weak. I was given the chance to be with them again and I didn't take it because I was scared. Scared of a little physical pain. The damn knife was so sharp I probably wouldn't have even felt the cut. *Damn!*" He slammed his fist against the steering wheel and then rested his head on the balled hand. He was still wearing the red mask, he realized. He pulled it off and tossed it to the floorboard, where it lay with the fallen invitation.

*What if it isn't too late?*

He restarted the car and swung it around in the road, throwing gravel and dust high and far behind him as he spun the tires and raced back toward the highway.

The eastern horizon was just beginning to turn gray as Lewis reached the warehouse again. He jumped from the car and ran to the door. It was locked. Lewis pulled until his arms ached, but to no avail. He returned to the car and fetched the tire tool. Within minutes, he had splintered the wood around the lock. The mechanism broke loose and fell to the floor inside the building. Lewis hurried through the office and into the warehouse area.

The vast room seemed darker. Only the pale light of the fading stars crept in through dirty windows set high in the walls. Lewis could barely see the tables. He started toward them.

"I'm back," he called to the empty chamber. "I've come to feed you. I want to be with you. Beth! Brandon!" There was no answer. Lewis felt his pointed tail swishing behind him as he walked. He was now close enough to see that something large was laying on the top of one table.

It was the body of a man. A derelict, Lewis guessed by the shabby dress and stench of stale, cheap alcohol that came from the corpse. In the pale light, Lewis could see the long gash in the man's throat. Not a drop of blood remained on the wound. Beneath the man's head, which hung over the edge of the table, just as his own should have done, Lewis saw the large punch bowl, now overturned. Only the faintest smear of crimson gave evidence of what had been contained therein.

Lewis began to weep again. "It should have been me," he moaned. "It should have been me." He began hitting the corpse, pounding the lifeless body as if the tramp were the one to blame for his failure.

Beth and Brandon, his own wife and son, had been forced to take sustenance from this nameless bum, he thought. *Forced to feed from society's waste all because their husband and father was too weak to give them what they needed.* He threw his head back as a sob tore from his body and tears streaked his face.

A powerful beam of light hit Lewis full in the face and he staggered back, his arm raised to ward off the illumination. "Hold it right there, buddy!" A man's voice echoed throughout the warehouse. Lewis saw the gun in the man's hand and a glint on the badge pinned to his chest. Had there been an alarm system activated by the breaking of the lock?

"What is it, Bill?" Another man entered the building.

"Somebody dressed as the devil," the fist cop answered. "And it looks like a body on the table there."

"You! On the floor." The second policeman approached Lewis, motioning with his gun for him to lie down.

"You don't understand," Lewis began. *Why bother to explain?*

"On the floor, now!" The cop was moving closer.

"I'm coming, Beth," Lewis whispered. He could feel the chill spot in the palm of his hand where Brandon had held him. Was the hand there again, pulling him forward, begging him to play, to run, to go fishing?

Lewis broke into a run, a smile on his face, the image of a small, green catfish splashing in a river as it was pulled to shore urging him on as he heard his wife's laughter and squeals of delight ringing in his ears.

He didn't hear the exclamation of surprise from the policeman barring his exit. He didn't feel the impact of the bullets as they slammed his body to the floor.

"Hi, Daddy."

He heard Brandon's voice and felt the soft, loving touch of his wife as she helped him up and into a new world of shadows.

# SKN-3

Children crowded the dirty street, some carrying bags or sacks of treats given by local residents, or stolen from other children in other parts of the borough. Older kids sat on the curb smoking pot or whatever their pusher sold them last. No mothers would call these kids home as the evening grew steadily darker. Screams filled the night, but that was not unusual for this neighborhood. Jack-o-lanterns that had not yet been smashed by the marauding children of the ghetto still glowed dully in the dirty night.

Reluctantly, the trick-or-treaters and drug users and pushers moved aside to let a battered old Mercury chug past them.

The long brown Mercury stopped in front of the house where Dr. Daniel Stillson had set up his medical practice. A tall white man got out from the driver's side and a huge Negro from the passenger side. The black man opened a back door and began pulling another white man from the seat. The driver came around the car to help his companion.

The man they extracted from the car was unconscious. He was well-dressed, in a tailored gray suit, though his silk tie had come untucked from under his suit coat and flapped in the gentle breeze as the other two men, supporting him between them, dragged him through the yard to the front door of Dr. Stillson's home office. A scowling jack-o-lantern watched them from inside the window.

Once on the porch, the black man knocked heavily on the front door. A curtain in the window flickered before the door was pulled open and the three men admitted. The door closed quickly behind them.

"Bring him in here," Dr. Stillson said, waving for the other men to follow him. Daniel Stillson was a medium-sized man of about forty-five, though he looked at least ten years older due to life in the city's slums. He was losing his dark hair at the crown, but his eyes still burned with unspent life. Tonight they shone even brighter than usual. Tonight he was a man on the brink of revenge.

The doctor led his guests into his examination room, the cleanest room in the house, and also the kitchen. White linoleum covered the floors, and the many cabinets on the walls were painted white, though in many places the paint was faded and stained. The sink in the corner had rust stains around the drain, and the table where the doctor sat to talk with his patients was propped up by chipped bricks because one of the legs had been broken off by a patient who had gotten angry over a price. The only other piece of furniture in the room was the steel examination table, and it was unremarkable except for the fact that tonight it was equipped with pieces of nylon rope tied to each of the four legs.

"Undress him and put him on the table," Dr. Stillson instructed. "Then tie his wrists and ankles with those ropes. Make sure you get them tight. Stretch him out so he can't move." He stood by and watched as his orders were carried out. When he was satisfied, he tossed a bottle of pills to each of the two men.

"Remember," he warned, "You don't know anything."

"Right," they both agreed.

"Good. Now go." Stillson followed the two and locked the door behind them. He heard the cough and roar as the old Mercury was started and driven away. He peeked out the window again to make sure his visitors had not attracted any unwanted attention.

Just the usual scum, he decided. The little ones dressed in costumes were less monstrous than their reality tonight. He let the dingy curtain drop back into place and returned to the examination room.

He stood over the unconscious body on his table for a few minutes, studying the smooth, pale flesh and the peaceful look of the handsome face. Then, smiling to himself, he turned and walked away.

From a corner, he pulled out a small, wheeled cart with a gleaming metal tray for a top. He removed the utensils he would need from a drawer: a scalpel, a syringe, and a new needle in a plastic wrapper. He took a small, corked bottle of clear liquid from a cabinet and placed all these items neatly on the tray of his cart and pushed them to the examination table. He brought a chair from the conference table and put it beside the tray, then sat down to wait for the man to regain his senses.

The wait wasn't long. The man's head began to move, his well-groomed blond hair becoming mussed. He tried to raise an arm, and the ropes held it down. His head snapped up and he found Dr. Stillson's smiling face. The man's eyes widened in surprise.

"Hello, Jeffrey," Dr. Stillson said. "Or shall it still be Mister Davies? Like it was in the courtroom? No, I think here it will be just plain old Jeff. Is that all right with you?"

"What am I doing here, Stillson?" Jeff demanded. "Where the hell am I?"

"Why, Jeff," the doctor feigned surprise. "This is my new office. Don't you like it? It's the best I can do since you ruined my practice with that nasty law suit."

"You killed my wife," Jeff accused, again.

"It was an accident," the doctor said harshly. "I explained before the operation that there was the chance she wouldn't make it through. You didn't hesitate to give me the go-ahead."

"You killed her because she wouldn't have sex with you in the hospital room."

Dr. Stillson's face reddened. "She was mine. She needed me as much as I wanted her. You should have heard her begging me to fuck her that first day she came to me. She said her husband was too busy with his work at the bank to give her the dick when he came home, if he came home. She told me she had heard rumors of homosexual activity between you and a clerk in the vault. Did you like getting corn-holed while you were bent over stacks of hundred dollar bills? Huh, Jeffy?"

"Fuck you! Why am I naked? Where are my clothes?"

"They've been taken care of. Be happy with what you have on.

"I made love to Molly," Stillson confessed. "You never got me to admit that in court, did you? No. But I did. She was a wonderful lover. Exquisite, really. She was going to leave you before we found out the lump was cancerous. I wanted her to leave you immediately then, but she didn't want to go through a divorce until after the operation. We made love in her hospital room several times. Even after her hair fell out.

"I miss her," Dr. Stillson added. "I doubt you do."

"It's none of your business," Jeff said. "Why am I here?"

"I'm going to do an operation on you tonight, Jeff. I've never performed this particular operation on a human before, but I'm sure if Molly were here she would give me the okay, just like you did for her. Besides, you're not that much different than an animal. Are you?"

"You're not going to cut on me," Jeff said. "You can't."

"Sure I can," Dr. Stillson said. He plucked the scalpel from his tray and showed it to his patient. "I'm all ready to go."

"No," Jeff said quietly. "No! Help! Somebody help me!"

"Nobody will help you because nobody cares!" Dr. Stillson shouted over the other man's voice. "We're in the slums, Jeff. The ghetto. The people out there, they've heard shouts coming from this house before. Most of my patients are thieves, gang members and their ilk. My neighbors won't care about your shouts."

"Nooo," Jeff moaned.

"Oh, yes," the doctor said in a reassuring tone. He took the syringe and the needle from his tray and fitted them together. He picked up the small bottle and stuck the needle through the cork, pulling the plunger up until the syringe was just over half full. He put the bottle back on the tray and shot a quick stream of the clear fluid into the air.

"Got to get the air bubbles out," Stillson said. "I don't want you dying of a heart attack. I have something much better in mind."

"What is that?"

"This?" Dr. Stillson brandished the syringe. "This is a concoction that I made up. I call it SKN-3. The three is because the first two tries were unsuccessful. It's an amphetamine. Speed. Can you say trick-or-treat? I thought you could."

"Don't …" Jeff whined as Dr. Stillson brought the needle close to his arm. He winced as the steel penetrated his flesh. The plunger came down and the fluid was in his blood. "Now what?" Jeff asked, a tear coming from his eye.

"Now we wait," Dr. Stillson said, dropping the empty syringe onto the tray. "It should be just a few seconds before the drug takes effect."

"Then what?"

"Then, Jeff, I'm going to skin you alive. SKN-3 will keep you conscious for most of the operation. Won't it be interesting to watch as your flesh is peeled off?"

"*No!*" Jeff began yelling for help again. Dr. Stillson let him shout without trying to stop him. He sat calmly and watched his patient, smiling when he saw the drug was working. Jeff's eyes bulged in their sockets and his face turned red as if he were blushing deeply. He trembled slightly. His heart beat rapidly beneath his skin, causing the flesh of his chest to pulsate.

"My hair's crawling," Jeff said. "Are there bugs in it?'"

"No, it just feels that way," the doctor told him. "I think we're ready to begin." He stood up, pushed the chair out of his way, lifted the scalpel from the tray, and pushed the cart back beside the discarded chair. He stepped close to the trembling man on his table.

"No. Please. I'll give you anything," Jeff begged, his voice hoarse with fright. "Anything you want."

"All I want from you, Jeff, is revenge," Dr. Stillson said. "And I'm about to have it."

Jeffrey Davies howled when the cold steel of the scalpel touched his super-sensitive skin. Dr. Stillson ignored the noise and concentrated on his cutting. He made an incision from a point a few inches below the Adam's apple to just above the start of the pubic hair. The cut swelled with ripe, red blood that soon spilled from its canal and ran down the man's hairless chest and stomach. Jeff continued to shriek with pain, and the doctor smiled to himself as he made his next cut along the inside of the left arm, then the right, and then the legs. He joined the slits on Jeff's limbs to the first cut on his torso, and peeled the flesh away from the carcass. Jeff's screams became louder and shriller, reaching an octave that Dr. Stillson would have believed impossible coming from the human throat.

Jeff's ropy red muscles glistened beneath the room's naked hundred-watt bulb. Within moments after his insides were exposed, Jeff passed out. Dr. Stillson looked at his watch.

"Good," he judged. "You stayed awake for the best parts, Jeffy. Thanks to my little drug."

The doctor completed his job, his face a mask of concentration. He cut from the top of his first incision, below the Adam's apple, around the base of the neck as far as he could reach. He untied Jeff and rolled the body over so he could complete the cuts on the wrists and ankles, then, bringing the cut from the man's neck up around the hairline and back to the forehead.

Taking hold of Jeff's blond hair, Dr. Stillson pulled slowly and steadily. The scalp lifted, and with a little help, the rest of the man's flesh came away from his back with a wet, sucking sound. Dr. Stillson lifted the skin away from the calves carefully so as not to tear the trophy, and then spread the dripping hide on his floor, inside up.

Leaving the body on the table for a moment, the doctor went to a cabinet and took out several white rags. He knelt beside his prize skin and wiped away the blood. When the inside was clean, he flipped the hide over and wiped the streaks of crimson from the front.

The skinless body still glistened wetly on the table. Dr. Stillson stood looking at it for a long moment. He smiled. "Happy Halloween, Jeffy," he said. "I love your costume."

He brought a bone saw from a drawer and quickly and expertly cut the body into small pieces, which he put into two Hefty Cinch Sacks along with the bloody rags. He then cleaned up his examination table and the floor around it, added these rags to the plastic bags, and closed them up. He pulled them to the far corner of the room to wait until he could hire a couple of junkies to dispose of them. Happy with a job well done, the doctor looked down at the skin laid out on the floor.

"I feel better, Jeff," he said. "Thank you." He took the small bottle of SKN-3 from the tray and examined the remaining fluid. "And thank *you* for keeping him awake long enough to make my task thoroughly enjoyable." He tossed the glass vial into the air, holding his palm out to catch it.

The bottle went up, tumbling end over end, and began its descent. The fluid within rolled from cork to bottom and back as gravity demanded. The bottle hit Dr. Stillson's upturned palm and bounced up before he could close his fingers around it. Again the bottle sailed through the air. It hit the skin stretched on the floor and shattered on impact with the hard linoleum beneath. Glass fragments flew like sparks in all directions as the liquid spread in a small stain.

"Shit!" The doctor glared at the mess. He stooped and picked the pieces of glass off the skin and the floor, then went for another rag to wipe up the formula. When he returned, the SKN-3 had soaked into the hide, leaving a small stain that looked like a birthmark.

"Oh well," Stillson said, "I suppose I didn't need the rest of it anyway." He dropped the rag onto his table and left the room, turning out the light.

He went to his bathroom and quickly showered, then to his bedroom and lay down, wearing only his underwear. He was asleep within minutes.

In his examination room, the skin began to move. At first the activity was only in the area where the fluid had stained the hide, a small rippling motion. Soon, however, the movement traveled outward until the entire hide was flowing, wave-like, from the headless scalp to the feetless legs and handless arms. The rippling became concentrated, and the skin began to inch its way across the floor toward the open doorway.

In the living room of the house it rolled itself into a turn and rippled past a worn chair, the outstretched arm brushing the leg of an end table. The jack-o-lantern in the window took no notice. The skin slithered into a short hallway and then over the threshold of Daniel Stillson's bedroom. It crossed the hardwood floor and was soon at the foot of the narrow bed. Snake-like, it raised itself up until the scalp seemed to be peeking over the edge of the bed. The top part of the skin flopped down onto the mattress and pulled the bottom of the torso and the legs up after it.

The skin quickly covered Dr. Stillson's nearly naked body, wrapping the empty husks of its arms and legs around the sleeping doctor. It began to squeeze.

Daniel Stillson woke up slowly, thinking at first that some of the neighborhood heavies had broken in and wanted drugs. He would give them something that would knock them on their asses for disturbing him. He looked through bleary eyes and saw the skin of Jeffrey Davies wrapped around him. He screamed.

The piece of flesh on the top end of the hide flopped forward. Dr. Stillson sucked Jeff's starchy hair down his throat and gagged.

As the doctor fought to free himself from the skin, the empty hide wrapped itself tighter around him, hugging out the small breaths he could draw around the hair in his throat. At last he lay still, his body limp, his gray eyes like specks of polished glass staring at the water-stained ceiling.

The skin continued squeezing for several hours, until all of Dr. Stillson's drug, the SKN-3, had evaporated from the flesh.

# Hungry is the Night

"Say that again," Rob Price said. He held the phone to his ear and listened to the woman as he scrawled on a notepad.

*Valerie Coon – Jogging on Pole Rd 5:30 a.m., ran through dark patch, came out exhausted. Skin was dry. Scared. Something in the dark.*

"Did you go to a doctor?" Rob asked.

"Well, no," Valerie answered. "What would I tell her?"

"Same thing you told me," Rob suggested. "So, tell me, why are you calling the newspaper about this? Did you call the police?"

"Yes, I did, and they were no help at all," she said, her prim voice becoming indignant. "Sergeant Ramsey was very rude about the whole thing."

"He thought it was a Halloween joke, didn't he?" Rob asked. He realized he was doodling spirals on his notepad.

"That's exactly what he thought. I am forty-three years old. I think I've seen a thing or two in my life and I am well past playing jokes on Halloween," the caller said.

"Yes, ma'am, I'm sure you are," Rob said. "So, this thing you ran through, it was on the road? Did it stay there?"

"It's gone now," she said. "It's daylight now."

"Of course." Rob dropped his pen and looked at the clock mounted above the front door of the newspaper office. It was almost three p.m. Lunchtime. He checked the name on his pad again, then said, "Listen, Miss Coon, I'll look into this and see what I can find out. I appreciate you calling. Bye now." He hung up, realized he'd broken his own rule by not asking for a call-back number, then shrugged. No way he was calling her back.

"Sounded like a fun call," Christa McCurtain said from her desk across the room. "The Boogey Man made an early appearance in Harvest Hill?" She pushed up her green-rimmed glasses and grinned at him.

"Yep. Gave a middle-aged MILF jogger some chills and a rash," Rob said. "I say good for him."

"She's not a bingo player?" Christa joked.

"Guess not," Rob answered. He knew Christa's assignment for the day – writing a story about the interfaith bingo game held at the Community Center the middle of November every year – was not the Pulitzer Prize piece the twenty-three-year-old had envisioned when she graduated from community college with an associate's degree in journalism. A few years at the Harvest Hill Herald and she'd probably either get pregnant, give up the dream, or, if she was lucky, move on to a bigger town. They never lasted long.

"It's about three," Christa noted. "You going to lunch?"

"Yeah. If Greg shows up, tell him to get cracking on that football homecoming insert. We sold enough ads for a six-pager. He should have plenty of material."

"I'll tell him," Christa promised.

Rob sighed. Greg Hipson, a high school senior, already held the position of sports editor. That's how hard it is to get help, Rob mused. At least Greg knew the difference between an action verb and an adverb, and he took decent photos.

"Okay. I have my cell if you need me," Rob said. He saved the front page spread he was working on, then heaved himself out of his desk. *Maybe I should go jogging up Pole Road.* His knees popped and cookie crumbs rolled down the swell of his belly and committed suicide on the worn carpet.

"Enjoy that burger," Christa said, returning to her bingo story. The mayor, who also owned the town's only jewelry store, had promised to donate a diamond dinner ring to this year's game.

* * *

Cynthia, the bubbly mid-forties waitress, had scarcely turned away from Rob's table before his cell phone rang. Rob looked longingly at the tall burger with a quarter-slice of tomato peeking from under a bun as he fished the phone out of his pocket. No need to check the caller ID. "What's up, Christa?" he asked.

"Well, I'm sorry to bother you, but I just heard on the police scanner that Josef Higgins ran into something strange on his farm."

"What kind of strange?" Rob lifted the top bun and looked at the mustard spread on it, then at the strips of bacon resting on a bed of lettuce with the tomatoes keeping it all off the first slab of greasy meat.

"He was looking for one of his dogs that didn't show up for feeding this morning and found something like a cloud in a patch of woods on his place. He said it attacked him," Christa said.

"Attacked him?" Rob put the bun back on top of his burger, got Cynthia's attention and waved her over. "Can I get a to-go box for this? Gotta run."

"News biz?" Cynthia asked, grinning at him.

"That's what he reported," Christa said.

Rob nodded while he said into the phone, "I'll be back in a few minutes. Keep listening to the scanner. See if you can pick up anything else." He dropped some bills on the table and transferred his burger and fries into a Styrofoam box after taking one quick bite, then left the diner.

Back in his office, Rob fell into his chair, opened his burger and took another bite, then snatched up his phone and punched in the number for the police station. "Hey Irene, is Leon around?"

"He just got back from lunch," the old lady dispatcher said. "I'll put you through, Rob."

"Ramsey," a male voice proclaimed a moment later. Sgt. Leon Ramsey handled all media inquiries for the paper now because a pit bull attack had left him walking with a limp two years ago. He was also in charge of the station during the night shift.

"Leon, it's Rob. What's going on with Josef Higgins today?"

"You're on that scanner again, ain't ya?" Leon asked.

"Part of the job."

"Don't really know yet," Leon answered. "We got a unit out there, but no word back on what happened."

"What did he report?"

"Oh, something weird." Rob heard papers shuffle, then Leon read to him. "Found a black fog in the woods while he was looking for a lost dog. Says the fog moved toward him, caught him and he was disoriented."

"Disoriented?" Rob asked.

"Well, Josef's exact words were, 'It was like I was all fucked-up drunk'. I didn't think you'd want to write that."

"Let me do the paraphrasing," Rob said as he scribbled on his notepad.

"Yeah. He says he fell down, crawled around and finally got out of that shit – his words – but was tired as a motherfucker – again, his words."

"That it?"

"Well, says now he's got a real bad case of crotch-itch," Leon said. "You know, dry skin? Says it's all over, but it's his crotch that's really bothering him."

"You had any other calls like this?" Rob asked, still writing. Christa wasn't even pretending to work on her bingo story.

"Nope."

"You're sure?"

"You know something, Rob?"

"Valerie Coon called less than an hour ago with a similar story," Rob said.

"No shit?"

"Yeah. You'll let me know what you find out with Higgins?"

"Sure. You get any of those free movie passes lately?"

Rob stuck a French fry in his mouth. "Nah, not lately. I'll hook you up when I get something, though. Thanks, Leon." He hung up and related the missing details to Christa.

Greg Hipson came in a few minutes later, his iPod playing rap music so loud it seemed to be leaking out his nose. "Rob! My little sister wants you to run a story about her cat!"

Rob glared at the kid, then pointed to his own ears. Greg got the hint and popped the buds out of his hearing holes.

"Sorry, man," Greg said, pulling the white iPod out of his jacket pocket. The monotonous bass beat died suddenly. "My sister's kitten died. She wants a story about it."

"Won't happen," Rob said, turning his attention to his cold lunch. "Did you get those coaches' pictures taken?"

Rob felt Christa's dirty look before she said, "What happened to Kelsey's kitten?"

"It died," Greg said.

"No shit," Rob muttered.

"Eat, boss-man," Christa said. "How'd it die?"

"Don't know," Greg said. He pulled the old chair with the broken arm from its place at his small desk and dropped himself onto it. "She found it on the porch after school. It was dead. Mom said its hair is falling off and its skin is all rough and dry."

Rob stopped, his hand halfway to his mouth like a pincushion of fries. "Greg, don't you live next to the Higgins farm?"

"Yeah. He's a crazy old fart. He tried to tell my old man – "

"Was the cat sick?" Rob interrupted.

"Nah. It was fine this morning."

"What are you thinking, Rob?" Christa asked.

"Nothing. I don't know. This dry skin business. They all have dry skin."

"All who?" Greg asked. Christa caught him up quickly. "Man, that is fucked up. You think they might all be connected?"

Rob shrugged. Christa shrugged. They went back to work.

* * *

The afternoon wore on and evening slipped around the houses of Harvest Hill like flood water around stones. Rob rubbed his eyes and looked at the clock. It was nearly six p.m. He checked the front page spread he'd been working on and decided it was good enough. There was a black box above the fold for a big photo.

"Christa, you're getting the trick-or-treat pics, right?" Rob asked.

"Yeah. I was just thinking I should get going," she answered.

"Probably so. Hit the Community Center, all the churches that turned in Halloween – sorry, fall festivals – and get shots of the kids there. I'll need them first thing in the morning."

"I know the drill," she said, shutting down her Mac and checking the batteries in her digital camera.

"I hope kids are dressed in scary costumes this year," Greg chimed in. "None of that Transformers or Disney princess crap. Where are the zombies and vampires and shit, man?"

"The churches won't let them in dressed like that," Christa answered, getting up and heading for the door. "See you guys tomorrow."

Before she got out the door the police scanner squawked to life again. Irene asked Unit 3 (of the city's five) to investigate at Bernice Miller's house. "She says something killed three of her chickens," Irene explained.

"Roger that," another female voice responded. It was Kelcee Gibson, Harvest Hill's only female cop.

"Chickens now?" Greg asked.

"Leon never called me back," Rob remembered. "I think I'll just mosey over there and see what's going on."

"Think he's still there?" Christa asked.

"It's Halloween. Harvest Hill is small, be we have teenagers. Teenagers plus Halloween equals pranks. Every employee HHPD has will be working tonight. Tomorrow'd be the day to rob the banks," Rob said.

He followed Christa out, telling Greg to wrap up his page and lock up when he left. Christa got in her Ford Focus and headed for the Community Center. Rob pulled out the keys to his Silverado, then paused. He decided to walk, since the police station was just two blocks north and around the corner. Still, despite the cool air, he'd worked up a sweat when he got there.

"What are you doing here this time of day?" Irene asked as she looked him over. She was a tiny woman with tall hair and half-rim glasses she peered over most of the time.

"Came to see Leon," Rob said, trying not to pant.

"He's in his office."

Rob went around Irene's desk. He found Leon, a stout man in his early thirties with a buzz cut, sitting at a desk cleaning a semi-automatic pistol.

"Rob, I completely forgot to call you back," Leon said, lowering the body of the weapon with a rod sticking from its barrel. "Sorry about that."

Rob waved him off and collapsed into one of the hard wooden chairs across the desk from the cop. He sighed, then asked, "So, what was it?"

"Don't know. We didn't find anything. There were no signs of violence. You know, didn't look like anybody'd roughed him up. Eddie Snyder checked it out, told him to quit drinking before noon, keep his dogs home and take a bath in baby oil for the dry skin."

"Humph," Rob grunted. "What about this new one? The chickens?"

Leon shrugged and began slowly moving the silver rod up and down in the barrel of his gun. "Three dead chickens. Could be a coyote. Maybe a fox or weasel."

"Is the skin dry?"

Leon stopped cleaning and looked at him. "I don't know."

"Can you call Kelcee and ask her to check?"

Still looking at Rob, Leon reached for a radio microphone. "Unit 3, do you copy?"

"Copy that, Leon. What's up?" Kelcee asked. She was a pretty young thing, in her late twenties with hair like summer wheat. Rob thought about her a lot.

"Have you arrived at the Miller place yet?" Leon asked.

"Just pulled up to the house," she responded.

"Call me on your cell," Leon said, then put the mic back. A moment later his cell phone played the James Bond theme song. "Listen Gibson, I want you to do something while you're checking into this one. See if the chickens' skin is dried out." He paused. Rob couldn't make out the words, but recognized the quizzical tone coming from the earpiece of the phone. "Just do it, okay?" Pause. "Thanks." He hung up and faced Rob. "So?"

"I told you about Coon calling me. Then there was

Higgins. That boy I have working for me, Greg Hipson, shows up and says his sister's cat was killed. Fur was falling off the body and the skin was real dry, he said. He lives next to Higgins. Now we have Bernice Miller."

"We've had a pretty dry spell here lately," Leon said.

"Uh-huh. You don't see it, do you?"

"You're gonna have to spell it out for me, Rob," Leon confessed.

"Coon is about two miles outside of town. Higgins is what, one mile? Greg's family's on Route 10, half a mile from the city limits, and the Millers are just on the edge of town. It's pretty much a straight line from Coon to Miller."

"So?"

"You don't think it's weird all these people are having things happen that involves dry skin?" Rob insisted.

"We don't know there's any eczema going on at the Millers'."

"If there is?"

"What? You think there's a rash monster out there? We have a ditzy flirt, to be nice to Ms. Coon, plus a drunk, a kid who let her kitten out of the house, and some dead chickens. Another half hour into trick-or-treating and Mrs. Miller would have had to wait until morning to get a cop out there. As it is we just sent Gibson."

"Because a girl cop isn't like a real cop?" Rob asked. "Good thing we're off the record right now, huh?"

"Come on, Rob," Leon pressed.

"I want to know if Miller saw that black fog, too," Rob said. "Coon said she saw it. So did Higgins."

"Higgins probably saw a shady patch under a pine tree and Valerie Coon wouldn't know fog from chocolate pudding," Leon said.

"What if there is something to it?"

"I don't see it as a possibility."

Rob huffed. "You're kidding?"

"One of the things you're talking about hasn't even been reported to us, Rob. You're asking me to make an illogical conclusion based on things we haven't even investigated."

"All right, Mr. Spock," Rob conceded. "Wouldn't want you to get illogical. Anything else going on? Windows soaped, houses egged?"

"Nope."

"Well, it's early."

"That it is," Leon agreed.

As if on cue, they both turned toward the small window in Leon's office. The evening had deepened. The few passing cars had their headlights on and the downtown businesses that passed out candy to the kids were shining brightly. A few kids were already out, carrying plastic pumpkins, pillow cases and Wal-Mart sacks to collect their treats.

"I remember one year, me and Sam Mitchell and a few others found unlocked cars and wedged sticks between the front seat and the horn buttons," Leon said, still watching out the window. "We did that all over town. Nobody ever figured out it was us."

"You're confessing that to a newspaper man," Rob reminded.

Leon snorted and turned away from the window. "Old news," he said.

"Gives me an idea for next year, though. Halloween pranks respectable adults did as kids," Rob said. "That could be fun."

"If you could get anybody else to admit it. Small towns have long memories, you know."

"Tell me about it. Old Lady Hutchison still – "

The police radio blared to sudden life as Irene ordered Units 1 and 2 to report to 153 Walnut. Her voice was tight and commanding, not at all the laconic old lady voice she usually used. Both Leon and Rob looked at each other. A moment later the woman herself was in Leon's door. She started to speak, then looked sidelong at the newspaper editor.

"Go ahead, Irene," Leon said.

"Dead baby," she blurted. "Lily Sanderson's new baby, Emily. She took it trick-or-treating with Dusty, her first grader, and some of his friends and Jessica Bell. It was Jessica that called just a minute ago. Said they was crossing that field there on Walnut by her house and this black fog come up on 'em. She said it stuck to them, like spider webs. They tried to run, but the fog stuck to them. She said they couldn't see nothing in it. Kids was screaming, Lily was screaming and the baby was crying, then the black stuff separated and moved away from them, but that baby was dead right there in its mama's arms."

"Jessica told you all that?" Leon asked.

"Yes, sir," Irene answered. "Took me a while to get that much 'cause she was so hysterical. Lily's still screaming, too, and I could hear those kids carrying on like the devil himself was nipping their toes."

"I bet you that baby has dry skin," Rob said. "I bet they all do."

Leon just stared at him, but Irene asked, "Dry skin?"

"Never mind, Irene," Leon said. "Rob, want to take a ride with me?"

"You bet your ass I do."

"Just a sec." Leon got on the phone and called one of the investigating officers. "Gene, you call me ASAP when you get there. I want to know the condition of that baby's skin. Watch the others. See if they're itching or complaining about a rash or dry skin."

The two men got in Leon's patrol car and hadn't even pulled away from the curb when a radio call came through for an ambulance to come to Lily Sanderson's address. A moment later Leon's cell phone rang. He pulled it off his belt and put it to his ear. "Talk to me, Gene. What's going on?"

Rob tried to hear, but couldn't make out the words. He sat in the motionless car and waited. Finally, Leon hung up.

"I'll be fucked," Leon said, closing the phone.

"Are you going to tell me or not?" Rob demanded.

"Baby's skin is like sandpaper it's so dry. All of them. Gene said they're all itching and drinking like crazy. Dehydrated. That's why he called the ambulance."

"Damn." Rob wiped at his face, felt his jowls moving under his sweaty fingers. "Her address? It's on the edge of town?"

"Yeah."

"Are we going?"

For answer, Leon spurted away from the curb and they hurried through the downtown area, up Main Street as the businesses, then the bigger houses fell away behind them.

"There's the field," Leon said, slowing the cruiser to a crawl. He turned on the spotlight outside the car door and shined it over the field of high, dead grass gently waving in the dark. There was nothing unusual about the field.

A moment later another cruiser pulled up beside Leon's. Gene Rollo rolled down his window and asked Leon, "You see anything?"

"Nope. We just got here. Wanna check it out?"

The two cops agreed, parked their cars and all three men got out, the cops armed with flashlights, both vehicles' spotlights pointed toward the darkest edge of the field. Leon warned Rob to stay back and be careful where he walked.

They didn't have to investigate for long before Leon called them all over to a place near the street on the east end of the field. "Look here," he said. "There was a struggle."

Rob looked and saw how a lot of the tall grass was mashed down in one big area. Trails led away from that spot in various directions.

"I'd say this is where somebody crawled away," Gene commented, waving his light over a path with more flattened grass than the others.

"Yep," Leon agreed.

Rob met Leon's eyes and saw fear and realization in them. "What do you think, Rob?" the cop asked.

"I don't know. It seems this thing, whatever it is, is moving toward town. Toward more people," Rob said. Leon nodded.

"You want to tell me what's going on?" Gene asked.

"Damned if I really know," Leon said. He looked to Rob again and Rob shrugged. "Here's what we know," Leon began, then related what they'd put together so far. "Now it's killed someone."

"This some kind of Halloween joke?" Gene asked.

Leon only shook his head. "Sounds like a lot of – " He stopped mid-sentence, his eye locking onto something behind the other two men. "What the fuck?"

Rob turned and looked where the policeman was looking. On the west end of the field, where it was darkest, something was moving. The beams from the cruisers' spotlights were shining in that corner, furthest from the road, but there was something wrong. The beams seemed to be shrinking, as if the light was being swallowed. Then Rob was jolted by Gene as the burly cop pushed between him and Leon.

"I'll check it out," he said, his heavy flashlight raised to his left shoulder while he drew his gun with his right hand. He was several steps away from them before either Rob or Leon thought to act.

"Should we follow him?" Rob asked.

"I'm gonna check those lights," Leon answered. He hurried to his car as fast as his maimed leg would allow and adjusted the spotlight.

"My God," Rob breathed. The light fell on a solid mass of roiling blackness advancing over the field toward Gene Rollo, sucking up the light from his flashlight as they approached each other.

"It's somebody with some kind of weird fog machine," Gene called without looking back.

"I don't think so," Rob said, but his voice didn't carry.

"Gene, don't go in there!" Leon yelled.

It was too late, though. At the last moment, the policeman hesitated, unsure if he should proceed, but the moving cloud of darkness never paused. It slipped around him, wrapped him up and hid him from sight. But not from sound. His screams, high-pitched and very unmanly for such a solid-looking male, ripped through the night and Rob felt the hair stand up on his arms. Leon started by him, his gun drawn. Rob grabbed his arm.

"No. You don't know what's in there," Rob said.

"Let me go. He's – "

A shot rang out. The bullet zinged across the field and lodged into a tree across the street. Then another with no discernable destination. Gene screamed again, the shriek subsiding into a sustained wail of agony.

"Look!" Rob released Leon's arm and pointed at the black cloud.

"Good lord," Leon hissed.

"It's getting bigger, isn't it?"

"Yeah."

They stood silent for a moment, looking at the rolling mass of night, listening to their companion suffer, wondering what to do. Finally, Leon broke the moment by calling to his colleague.

"Gene! Can you hear me? What's happening in there? Can you tell me?"

The wailing broke for a moment. The two men waited for a response. The only sound was an anguished gasp, then the night was completely quiet.

"Get in the car," Rob whispered. "It's done with him."

He felt Leon looking at him, but didn't care. Rob edged backward, keeping his eyes on the dark cloud, a hand outstretched behind him, searching for the cool metal of the police car. He found it, felt around for the door handle, couldn't locate it, so risked a quick glance until he found it. He jerked the door open and scrambled inside. Leon got in the driver's side a moment later.

"We can't leave him out there," Leon said.

"No," Rob agreed. "But it sensed him there. It moved toward him. If we'd stayed out there, it might have come for us next."

"It might, anyway. Who's to say it can't get in here through the air vents or something?"

"It might," Rob agreed, still watching the black fog. It hadn't moved since Gene's final gasp, but now it seemed to rev up with motion, dark curls rolling and waving within it. Both men held their breath, watching, and finally the thing slipped away to the west, toward town, and the car spotlights showed a body in a dark uniform lying in the tall brown grass.

"Give it a minute," Rob warned, sensing Leon about to throw open his door. They waited, watching. The cloud moved through a chain link fence and into the backyard of a house.

"My God," Leon said. He grabbed his radio mic. "All available units!" he called. "This is Leon. I need you to turn on your flashers, drive up and down every street and order people back into their houses. Get everybody inside. Irene, you call the radio station and tell them to broadcast the warning. Everyone inside? Got it? Trick-or-treat is cancelled."

Irene's voice was sharp and professional. "Got it," she said.

Leon hung his head for a moment, then raised it and spoke into the mic again, summoning an ambulance to the field. "Officer down," he added. He looked to Rob. "You ready?"

They approached the fallen cop together. Gene Rollo

was motionless, face down in the tall grass, his eyes and mouth open. Leon's flashlight revealed the damage. Gene's lips were dry and cracked, his eyes dull, but not glassy. There was a white, chalky film on the skin of his face. Leon knelt and tried to roll the bigger man over. Rob dropped to his knees and helped turn Gene to his back. Leon pressed his head to Gene's chest.

"There's a heartbeat, but just barely," he said. He slapped lightly at Gene's face. The white powder flaked away.

Rob reached forward and touched the cop's face, scratching off some of the whiteness. "Dry skin," he said.

"Gene, can you hear me?" Leon asked over and over, still slapping the other man's face.

After a long while, there was a faint spark of recognition in Gene's eyes. He didn't move them, but his conscious thoughts were with the two other men and they recognized it.

"What was it?" Rob asked.

Gene's mouth moved, but there was no moisture. Leon leaned close, putting his ear to Gene's working mouth. Two syllables puffed out, then nothing else. The dim light faded from his eyes.

"What'd he say?" Rob asked.

Gene raised himself and looked at him. "Hungry."

They both looked down at the body again. "It's feeding on them," Rob said. "Like a vampire, but ... But it's taking all the moisture out of them. Not just the blood."

A moment later the ambulance was there. Leon and Rob didn't wait to see them drape a cloth other Gene's face. They were back in Leon's cruiser, heading for town with the emergency lights flashing red and blue. Leon used his radio microphone to broadcast through a loudspeaker, ordering people to stay indoors.

They'd covered several blocks when Leon's cell phone rang. He handed the microphone to Rob, then reached for the phone at his belt. "Keep it up," he said. "We have to keep people inside."

"Everyone, stay in your homes," Rob said into the mic, knowing his voice lacked the commanding tone and general volume of the cop's. Plus, he felt like he was in some bad B movie from the 1950s. *Some threat that is a metaphor for Communism is loose in our streets.* It would have been funny if there wasn't something even worse than the Reds really loose in town.

Leon put his phone back on his belt and took the mic away from Rob. "We have to go back to the station. Something's up and Irene can't make heads or tails out of what they're telling her."

"Who?"

"Your friend Valerie Coon is one of them." Leon goosed the accelerator and they flew through the empty streets, lights flashing and sirens screaming.

* * *

Inside the police station they found Valerie Coon, a tall, thin widow dressed in a witch costume with a plunging neckline and high hem, arguing with Deborah Griffith, a shorter, wider woman with a bob haircut and angry, flashing green eyes. Deborah's husband, Alan, stood aside, looking sheepish and, Rob was sure, not at all like the mill supervisor most people knew. The women were screaming at each other and Irene, from her place behind her desk, was yelling at them to shut up. The arguing women turned to face the two men as they entered, but Irene's view was blocked.

"Shut your fucking mouths!" Irene roared, her brittle old-lady voice full of blood and thunder. Rob clamped a hand over his mouth to hide the laugh that wanted to burst from him.

"What the hell is going on here?" Leon demanded.

"This hussy has been screwing my husband," Deborah accused.

"I didn't give him anything he didn't want," Valerie answered.

"How the hell is this police business?" Leon asked. Rob meandered to the side of the group, trying to go unnoticed, but he listened and watched. He kept looking at Alan, gauging his reaction to the accusations.

"It's police business because she tried to kill me," Valerie Coon answered. She turned on Rob. "I called you and told you about it. Turns out this little stick-up-her-ass bitch summoned that black cloud thing I told you about. It was supposed to kill me."

The room was silent for a long moment. Finally Rob spoke. "Is that true, Mrs. Griffith?"

"So what if it is?" she asked. "Didn't happen, anyway." She appeared to be a pouting child, crossing her short, chubby arms over her chest, her large yellow purse slapping against her stomach.

"My God," Leon said, his teeth gritted in rage. "You called that thing?"

"I don't think it even worked," Deborah huffed.

Leon grabbed her and spun her around to face him. Her arms uncrossed and her purse fell to the floor, spilling its contents. "It worked, you stupid fuck," Leon hissed at her. "Gene Rollo is dead. I saw him killed. We got a dead baby, too, plus a bunch of scared kids."

"Hey, don't treat my wife like that," Alan said, suddenly coming to life and stepping toward the cop.

Leon's hard eyes never left Deborah's face, but his left hand reached out and his index finger was a dagger pointing at the offended husband. "You stay put," he ordered. Alan stopped, dropped his raised hands to his sides and lowered his head.

"You mean it's true?" Valerie asked. "She sent that fog-thing after me?"

"There's something out there, and she's confessed to sending it," Leon answered.

Rob squatted and pulled a sheaf of papers from the makeup cases, keys and tissue that had come from Deborah's purse. "Here's how she did it," he said, wheezing as he rose to his feet. He read from the top page, "Summoning minor demons to do one's bidding," he said. "She's highlighted this heading. Dhargolmet: The Living Dark."

Leon snatched the papers from him and looked at it, then waved them under Deborah's nose. "This is it?" She didn't answer. "Where did you get this?"

"I got it off the Internet," she answered.

"How do you get rid of it?" Rob asked.

The haughty look vanished instantly from her face and she suddenly looked nervous. "You don't. Not until … not until it gets what it was called for. The instructions said there might be some collateral damage, but I thought since this whore was right down the road it would be okay."

With his left hand, Leon flung the papers away from

him while his right cocked back, the hand balled into a fist. Rob pushed himself between the cop and the woman. "Don't be stupid, Leon," he said. "You can't hit a civilian. A woman."

"It's her fault that baby and Gene are dead," Leon spat.

"Sounds like they're all guilty," Rob answered. He turned to Alan Griffith. "Did you sleep with Valerie?"

The man kept his eyes on the floor, but nodded almost imperceptibly. "Didn't mean any harm. Just … just wanted some fun."

"We had it, too," Valerie added.

"Whore!" Deborah lunged at Valerie, her hands outstretched like claws, and Valerie stepped into it, getting one good uppercut to the smaller woman's face before they both fell to the floor. The three men worked to pull them apart. Rob ended up with his arms around Valerie's middle, holding on for dear life for a minute before she calmed down and shrugged him off. Her dress had ridden up high enough he could see that she only wore a black thong under it. Alan held his wife despite the fact she gave his foot a solid stomping and demanded he let her go.

"All right," Leon said. "All right." He paced quickly around the small room.

"I'll tell you what you ought to do," Irene piped up, apparently over being embarrassed by her earlier vulgarity.

"What's that?" Leon asked.

"Put them all outside. Chain them up outside and let them reap the wages of their own sins," she said. "Let God protect the innocent, though I think innocent folks are all safe in their homes by now."

Rob snorted, but his mirth died when he looked at

Leon and realized the cop was seriously considering it. "You're not thinking about doing it," he said.

Leon ignored him and focused on Deborah again. "If this thing gets what it wants, the one you sent it after, it'll go away?"

Deborah nodded.

Valerie's face paled. "You will not," she said it like a dare, but her voice lacked conviction.

Leon turned to Rob. "My job is to protect and serve the people of Harvest Hill," he said. "Guns won't work against what we saw. Gord's didn't help him. If I can help everyone by sacrificing them, why not?"

"Your job is to enforce the law, not play judge, jury and executioner," Rob said.

"There's no time, man. You saw it," Leon argued. He reached to the back of his belt and pulled two sets of handcuffs out of pouches. "Irene, get me another set of cuffs," he called. The little woman hurried to obey.

"Leon," Alan finally spoke again. "Come on. What are you thinking?"

"I'm thinking I lost a good man and this town lost two citizens because of you three."

"This is nuts," Alan said, edging toward the door.

Leon drew his gun and pointed the black semi-automatic weapon at the man. "Step back over here or I'll shoot you where you stand."

Alan's face paled, but he moved back to join the group.

"Rob, I need you to cuff them," Leon said. "Put our Casanova between the two women and cuff their wrists together."

"I'm not doing that," Rob answered. "I don't want

any part in that. You just can't do it, Leon."

Leon's face remained emotionless, but his gun hand rotated so that the weapon was pointed at the newspaper editor. "You'll do it, Rob, and you'll shut the fuck up about it." His other hand offered the gleaming silver handcuffs. Rob took the restraints. "Do it," Leon urged.

Reluctantly, Rob put the cuffs on Alan's wrists, fastening the other ends to Valerie and Deborah.

"You won't get away with this," Valerie said.

"I think you're wrong," Leon answered. "When the people see that I acted in their best interests, I think they'll be okay with it."

Irene returned with another pair of handcuffs that she handed over to the cop. "Let's go outside," he said.

"What's out there?" Alan asked. "Really, what's out there?"

"Don't do this, Leon," Rob said.

"Let's go." Leon motioned toward the door with his gun. The prisoners shuffled forward. Deborah was at the front of the line and had to open the door. As she went through, Rob saw Alan lean forward and say something to his wife, then turn to his mistress. The trio broke into a run.

Leon fired his pistol once before the door closed. Rob knew he'd scored a hit. Alan cried out in pain and a bloodstain could be seen on the concrete outside the glass door. Rob followed Leon outside, where they found Alan on the sidewalk, clutching his right calf.

"Get up," Leon ordered, leveling the gun at Alan's other leg. The unfaithful husband pushed himself to his feet. "To the flagpole," Leon ordered.

Rob argued with the cop as they went to the flagpole

planted where the sidewalk joined the parking lot. Leon ignored Rob and ordered the three people to make a ring around the pole, then he closed the circle by handcuffing the women together.

"Everyone else in town should be inside," Leon said. "You're the only ones out here. If you make it through the night, I'll let you go."

"Please," Deborah begged. "Don't leave us out here for the demon."

Even Rob had a hard time feeling sympathy for the woman who'd called the thing. Leon ignored her and turned to Rob. "You staying out here with them, or coming back inside? Irene will make some fresh coffee."

Rob looked from Leon to the three people cuffed to the pole. Above their heads the American flag was too heavy to so much as flutter in the light breeze. Rob shook his head. "I'm not staying out here." He followed Leon inside.

* * *

"How're you going to write this up for the paper?" Leon asked as they sat in his office sipping coffee. His gun was holstered, but his eyes were accusing.

"I hadn't thought about it," Rob lied.

"Bullshit."

"I don't know, Leon. I don't know. This is just … I don't know."

"Leon! You better come out here," Irene called.

The two men hurried out of the office to the front of the station. It was completely black outside.

Irene was huddled behind her desk, trembling and clutching a tan sweater in front of her as she stared at the door. Rob followed her gaze and saw the heavy, oily black fog pressed against the glass.

Then the screams came from outside.

* * *

Rob pushed himself away from his desk and rubbed his eyes with an open hand, then looked at the new lead story on the front page of his computer monitor. The head stretched from side to side, proclaiming: TRICK-OR-TRAGEDY! The subhead was smaller: Local cop saves town from further terror. The sub-head wasn't totally necessary, but it filled space, added pizzazz and deflected … Rob had to pause as his ethics hiccupped somewhere deep in his gut. Deflected people from the truth, he finally admitted. He read his lead paragraph one last time:

Five Harvest Hill residents are dead and many others were treated for minor illnesses after a cloud of toxins seeped from a private well outside of town. The dark cloud moved into the city just after nightfall, cancelling trick-or-treat activity. Police Chief Leon Ramsey neutralized the toxic cloud with a CO2 fire extinguisher.

"God," Rob almost groaned. Had stealing the end of *The Blob* been going too far? "Fuck it."

The story wasn't completely false. The cloud had been deadly, and Leon was the man who'd stopped it. Nobody had seen the three bodies shackled and sacrificed beneath the lifeless American flag, so maybe the public would swallow this half-truth. Why not? They swallowed season after season of reality TV.

Rob reached out with a thick finger and clicked the computer mouse button, sending the PDF of the front page to the printing press the Herald shared with the nearby Clegg Valley Packet.

"No going back now," he muttered. "It's better this way. Better this way."

Laying on the desk beside his computer were the pages that had fallen out of Deborah Griffith's purse. *They should be shredded.* Instead, he put them in a manila folder and stuffed them in the back of his file cabinet.

# Scream of Humanity

The door of the little house burst open with such force that Dr. Paul Rutledge jerked, sloshing hot broth from the bowl he held. His father yelped and cursed on the bed beneath him. Paul looked from the door, where a boy in dusty clothes stood panting and bracing himself against the frame, to his father, his face scrunched up while he rubbed his neck where the broth had scalded him.

"Luke Groves!" Daniel Rutledge rasped from the bed. "Is that how your mother taught you to enter a house that ain't even your own?"

"No sir," the boy said between gasps. "I'm sorry, sir, but it's Ma. It's her time. She sent me for you."

The starch drained out of the elder doctor and he slumped back to his pillow. Paul looked again from the boy to his sick father. He set aside the broth and took up a cloth that he dipped into the wash basin near the bed.

"Here, Father, let me," Paul said, gently pulling his father's hand away from his burned neck. The tight, thin flesh was red and still wet with broth, but not blistering. Paul pressed the cool cloth over it, then let his father hold it in place. He turned back to the boy.

"Luke, is it?" Paul asked. The boy nodded. "Come in, son. Come in and catch your breath."

The barefoot boy – he couldn't have been more than ten years old – went to the rough plank table and slid onto the end of one of the benches. His eyes were wide, his blond hair a little too long and his whole body covered in a coat of country dust. His overalls were in need of fresh patches around the knees and were a couple of inches too short in the legs. The shirt he wore under the overalls was at least two sizes too big.

Paul moved away from the bed and took a dipper of water from a bucket near the stove. He offered it to the boy, who drank it greedily and handed it back empty. Paul gave him more and the boy drank again.

"Thank you," he said. "I'm real sorry about busting in your door like that. It's just that Ma needs the doctor." He looked back to the bed, then up at Paul. "Who are you?"

"I'm Paul. I'm Dr. Rutledge's son. I've been away at school for quite a while. I'm a doctor, too."

"Is he dying?" Luke asked, nodding toward the bed.

"Not today," Paul answered softly. "He's just got a chill from standing in the cold river with his bare feet."

"I do that all the time," Luke argued.

"You're not an old man who doesn't take proper care of himself," Paul answered, smiling and looking back to his father.

"The boy's ma is going to have a baby and you're calling me a foolish old man," Daniel wheezed. He turned his sallow face and watery eyes to the boy. "She's close to time?"

"Yes, sir," Luke answered, nodding vigorously. "She said she knows it's 'bout time."

The old man nodded once, then said, "You go saddle up the horse, Luke. Paul here will tend to your ma."

The two doctors watched the boy fly out of the house. The older man called his son over, waving him toward the stool near the bed.

"There are things they don't teach you in college, Paul," Daniel said, struggling for breath through his chest congestion. "Renea Groves is a smart enough woman, if not virtuous, and likely knows her time has come. But mark me, son, you need to get that baby birthed before the sun goes down tonight."

Paul stared at his father for a long moment, his brow wrinkled as he tried to make sense of the words. "Why is that?" he finally asked.

"There are times when and places where the invisible barrier between the worlds of the living and the dead are thin." Daniel watched his son for a moment, gauged his reaction, then shook his head. "You don't believe me."

"I know today is All Hallow's, but only the superstitious and Catholics mark the day, Father. Why are you telling me this about invisible barriers?"

Daniel opened his mouth to respond, but a coughing fit overcame him. Paul helped him to a sitting position, put another pillow behind him, and brought water. Daniel sat upright, wheezing and panting, unable to speak or even take the dipper. Luke reappeared in the doorway, holding the reins of the mare.

"Horse is ready, Doc," the boy said.

"Will you be all right here alone, Father?" Paul asked.

Daniel motioned his son to him, gripped his shoulder with a surprisingly strong bony hand and pulled the younger doctor close to wheeze into his ear. "If that baby isn't breathing, you smack it. If it still don't breathe, cover its head until dawn. Understand?"

Paul wanted to argue, but time was wasting and the boy was waiting.

"Sometimes," Daniel gasped, "Sometimes superstitions deserve attention. Be careful, Paul." The withered hand fell away and the old doctor slumped into his pillows. His breathing eased. He nodded. "I'll be fine. Go."

Paul backed toward the shelf where his shiny new black valise sat next to his father's faded and cracked bag. He took down his bag, still watching his father.

"Sir?" Luke urged.

"Go on," Daniel urged.

"I'll be home soon, Father," Paul said, then closed the door and mounted the horse, pulling the boy up beside him. They left at a gallop, heading south toward Benevolence, where the Groves lived on a small farm just outside the little eastern Oklahoma village.

"Has your mother's water broke?" Paul asked as they rushed along.

"I don't know what that means, sir. She just grabbed at her belly, said it was time and sent me to get the doc."

Except for some directions from Luke, they made the rest of the trip without speaking. At the Groves' cabin Paul helped the boy off the horse, then slid down himself and slapped some of the October dust off his clothes. The sun, well past noon, cast long dark shadows from the woods behind the house.

"Tend to the horse, will you, Luke?" Paul asked, handing over the reins. He took a deep breath, smelling wood smoke and autumn leaves and harvested land. Good smells he'd missed all those years he'd been away studying medicine in Atlanta. Gripping his valise, he went to the cabin, knocked briskly on the door, then let himself in.

The inside of the cabin was hot, clammy and smelled of human sweat. Gasps and cries of pain came from a corner of the main room that was partitioned off with hanging quilts. A haggard, weather-beaten man sat at a rough table on the opposite side of the room. He looked up from his hard hands when Paul entered.

"Mr. Groves?" Paul asked, though he recognized the farmer.

"Who're you?" the man asked.

"I'm Paul Rutledge. Daniel's son. My father is sick, so I came in his place. I'm a doctor, too."

"You brung babies?"

"Yes, I've delivered babies," Paul answered.

A scream ripped from behind the curtain. Floyd Groves slowly rotated his head to look at the hidden corner. "She's been screamin' like that for most of the day."

"I'll go check on her," Paul said.

"I got stock to tend," the farmer said. He slowly rose from his place at the table and left the cabin.

Paul pushed aside one of the quilts and stepped into the darkened area. Renea Groves lay in the bed, rolling from side to side and moaning, her wide, doughy face pale and glistening with a sheen of sweat. Bent over her was another wide-hipped woman. After a moment Paul recognized her as Katherine Bennett, a neighbor who lived down the road from the Groves. She'd had a son a year older than Paul, but he'd been killed by a bear. Mrs. Bennett seemed to feel his eyes on her and she turned to face him, wisps of her gray-and-brown hair hanging around her face like Spanish moss.

"What are you lookin' at? Who are you?"

"Paul Rutledge, Mrs. Bennett. Daniel's boy. I'm a doctor." He hoped this was the last time he'd have to repeat that litany. "Mr. Groves sent me in."

She nodded curtly, then asked, "Where's your pa?"

"He's sick. I've come instead."

"Well, get in here and help then," the woman ordered.

Mrs. Groves arched her back and howled in agony again. Paul stepped to the foot of the bed and put his satchel on the floor, then turned to a nearby basin and washed his hands in tepid water. He introduced himself again and offered rote words of comfort as he lifted the bottom of the blankets and inspected the pregnant woman.

"Can you get me some light?" he asked Mrs. Bennett.

She gave him a doubtful look, but lit an oil lamp and held it near him so he could better see the woman. He felt of her, then shook his head. "You have some time still, Mrs. Groves."

The woman eyed him suspiciously from her pillows without answering.

Grasping for comforting small talk, Paul asked, "Are you and Mr. Groves hoping for another son? Luke seems like a fine boy."

Mrs. Groves only glared at him. Mrs. Bennett snorted lustily. "Floyd Groves ain't the father," she said. "Everyone knows that. Mule kicked him in the balls six years ago and it ain't worked since then."

"Shut up!" Renea Groves shrieked. Paul looked from one woman to the other while they stared daggers at one another. "Ain't your business, you old busy body."

"It's everybody's business when a woman with a husband who ain't a man no more goes and gets herself with a baby," Mrs. Bennett responded.

"It's public knowledge that Mr. Groves was … injured like that?" Paul asked.

"Happened in the middle of town," Mrs. Bennett answered. "Mule just got tired of Floyd beating him with that stick. Waited until Floyd was behind him, then WHAM! Floyd like to have died from it. Couldn't walk for most of a month. Your pa treated him. Renea here complained all over town that her husband wasn't a man no more. Wouldn't sell that mule, though."

"I see," Paul said. He began to question his decision to return to rural Oklahoma. Working with Dr. Collins in Atlanta, tending to rich elderly ladies with mostly made-up maladies, hadn't been as colorful as the present situation, but he suddenly thought it hadn't been so bad. "Well, there's little we can do but wait this out," he said.

"You go on and sit at the table and I'll let you know when you're needed," Mrs. Bennett said.

"Thank you, but I think I'll check in at regular intervals, if that's okay with Mrs. Groves."

"I just want it out of me," the woman hissed. Paul nodded. Most women he'd tended during childbirth got like this as the time neared. Mrs. Groves' face contorted and she groaned deeply as her back arched again. How long since the last contraction? Five? Six minutes? It wouldn't be too much longer.

Paul went and sat at the table where the injured Mr. Groves had been when he came in. He took a medical pamphlet from an interior jacket pocket and read for a while, keeping an ear tuned to the agony of the pregnant woman. He checked her twice, but each time found her unready to deliver and returned to his reading until the room became too dim to see the words clearly. Paul looked up and realized the sun was setting behind the mountains west of the house.

*You need to get that baby birthed before the sun goes down tonight.*

His father's words made no more sense to him now than they had when the man first said them. Paul wondered how his father was doing and hoped he was resting.

"Doc, I think it's about time." Paul shook himself and turned away from the darkening window to find Mrs. Bennett looking at him from the partitioned room. "Come on," she urged.

* * *

"Push. You can do it, Mrs. Groves. Push … harder," Dr. Rutledge urged. The woman's knees were up, her feet digging into the tick mattress. The partitioned room smelled of perspiration and burning oil from the lamp. Mrs. Groves moaned and the young doctor tried to think of something soothing to say to her.

"It's the pain of guilt," Mrs. Bennett commented as she dabbed at her neighbor's strained, sweaty face. Paul wanted to ask why she was here if she had nothing better to say, but he didn't want to lose the help.

"Come on," Paul said to the pregnant woman. "You're doing fine."

The woman, bathed in sweat, groaned, her hands clawing at the sheet stretched over the mattress as she pushed hard enough to make the veins in her neck bulge. Dr. Rutledge stood at the foot of the bed, his hands trembling between the woman's thighs.

"Come on, Mrs. Groves, give it all you've got," he coaxed as the intensity of another contraction came over her.

The woman pushed. Her face contorted and a thin stream of excrement burst from her anus. Paul used one of the husband's ragged shirts to wipe her clean.

"Oh God, I shit myself," Mrs. Groves sobbed.

"Sure did," Mrs. Bennett confirmed in her condescending tone.

"That's okay," the doctor answered. "It happens. While we wait for the next contraction, I'm going to clean you up a little with this washcloth. It may feel cool." He took another cloth from a pile of rags heaped near the wash basin and wiped at the woman's nethers.

"How many babies you delivered?" Mrs. Bennett asked.

Paul paused, refused to look at her as he cleaned Mrs. Groves. "Several."

"You went to a fancy medical school?"

"Yes."

"You delivered them several babies by yourself, or did you have some teacher there tellin' you what to do?" she asked.

Mrs. Groves was silent.

Paul Rutledge finished cleaning his patient's ass and tossed the soiled rag into a corner. "I had instruction every time," he said as he moved to the wash basin to clean his hands.

"You've never did this by yourself?" Mrs. Groves asked in a tremulous voice.

Paul dried his hands and turned back to the women.

"I have done all the work, but always had an instructor standing by while I did it. You don't need to worry, Mrs. Groves. You're going to be just fine."

For an instant, her face showed doubt, then another contraction wracked her body and her face became a mask of pain.

"You ain't never delivered no baby 'round here, and especially not an Hallowe'en," Mrs. Bennett said.

"No, Mrs. Bennett, I have not," Paul said, his anger flashing. "But it makes no difference the time or place. Babies come all the time and everywhere in the world. Now, if you care to help, I am indebted to you. If you're only contributions are going to be sarcasm and cynicism, I'll thank you to leave me with my patient."

The doughty woman stared at him for a moment, then threw back her head and laughed deep from her ample belly. "I ain't going anywhere, Young Mr. Doctor," she promised. "You just go on about your business."

"Oh God!" Renea Groves screamed. She arched her back as another contraction came.

"I can see the head!" Dr. Rutledge said. "Push, Mrs. Groves, push."

She pushed. And screamed, and cursed. "I swear on my mama's grave I'll be a good Christian woman from here on," she raved. The skin between her vagina and anus began to tear. Dr. Rutledge grabbed his scalpel and sliced the skin with a steady hand. He smiled at the perfection of his cut. He'd never done that one before; the one time it had been necessary, Dr. Collins had done it. A bloody, hairy scalp appeared in the opening and he returned to business.

"You're doing it, Mrs. Groves," Paul said. "You're

doing fine."

She pushed one more time and Dr. Paul Rutledge eased the baby out in a slow corkscrew motion. He held the slimy, perfectly formed infant in his hands. *A boy!* He couldn't pull his eyes from the child – the first he had brought into this world on his own. He held the baby in one hand and deftly clamped the umbilical cord with the other. Almost half a minute passed before he realized the child had not yet drawn a breath and was not screaming. He looked at the eyes.

*If that baby isn't breathing, you smack it. If it still don't breathe, cover its head until dawn. Understand?*

"You better swat that baby's butt, Young Mr. Doctor," Mrs. Bennett warned, her voice serious, all traces of sarcasm and condescension gone now.

Paul started to turn the baby over to spank it, to see if the shock would cause it to suck in that vital first breath … but he hesitated.

"What is it you're afraid of?" he asked.

"This ain't no time to play around," Mrs. Bennett said stonily.

"Tell me," Paul insisted.

"Doctor?" the new mother's voice was weak and tired. Dr. Rutledge ignored her.

Mrs. Bennett glared at him. "Anyone knows that if a newborn baby don't draw breath right after it's born, you gotta make it breathe," she said. "The breath is what makes the soul. The baby'll start screaming once that first breath creates a soul inside its body. If you wait too long, evil spirits will find the baby and fill up the body. If that happens, the baby's eyes'll turn yellow and you got to strangle it and tell the mother it was born dead."

"Doctor?"

Paul looked from Mrs. Bennett to Mrs. Groves, who'd sagged into her pillows and looked exhausted, with dark circles under her eyes. Then he looked at the motionless infant in his hands. He turned it over and looked into its face.

Paul felt his own eyes widen as the dull eyes of the infant filled with an inner light. The eyelids fluttered, the child stared back at him, not with the blue-eyed newborn innocence of a baby, but with the gaze of something older. Nearly panicked, Dr. Paul Rutledge turned the baby over and swatted it on the buttocks.

No sound came from the child.

"Too late," Mrs. Bennett intoned. "Too late."

"Doctor? What's wrong?" the mother asked. "My baby's okay?"

*If that baby isn't breathing, you smack it. If it still don't breathe, cover its head until dawn. Understand?*

Paul struck the infant again. Nothing. The thing refused to so much as whimper or gasp. A burning red print showed where the doctor's hand had made contact. He turned the baby over. The eyes were dark.

*Not yellow!*

No, not yellow, but not right, either. The tiny face showed him a toothless grin as a slime-coated hand found his thumb and squeezed.

*There are times when the invisible barrier between the worlds of the living and the dead are thin.*

"Father, what have I done?" he whispered. "What have I allowed through?"

"Doctor?" Renea Groves struggled to sit up in the bed. "My baby? What's wrong with my baby?"

"You hush," Mrs. Bennett said. "That baby was born dead." The severe woman turned her attention to the doctor. "You gotta strangle it now. Strangle it or drown it."

Paul lifted his free hand, letting it hover over the pale body for a moment, then his fingers slipped under the chin.

*I can't do this … God, I can't do this …*

His fingers began to squeeze.

The curtain behind him fluttered and Mr. Groves' voice intruded into the delivery area, but was drowned out when the infant began to cry in a loud, lusty scream.

*What have I done?*

"Doc?" Mr. Groves asked.

Paul turned to face the man, the baby now kicking and squirming and crying in his hands.

"Give me that baby," Mrs. Bennett said. Paul turned back as the woman moved forward, her thick hands outstretched.

"No!" Mrs. Groves lurched forward, clutching at her child.

"I – I don't know what's going on here," Paul said. "Illegitimacy, mule kicks, and superstition. I don't know who the father of this baby is, and that isn't my business. The child is here now. I thought it was dead, but obviously it isn't."

"It ain't dead, but it's possessed by something that ain't supposed to be born a human baby," Mrs. Bennett hissed, still reaching for the squalling infant. Paul stepped away, found a small blanket that had been put aside for the baby and he wrapped the child in it and handed it to its mother. The child immediately quieted, its strange, old and dark eyes fixed on Paul.

Mrs. Groves gasped, her face twisted for a moment, then her placenta came out of her, making a glistening, gray-and-red blob on the bed. Paul looked at Mrs. Bennett and said, "Clean that up for me, please."

"Doc?" Mr. Groves tried again for his attention.

"Yes, Mr. Groves?"

"Fella's here to see you."

Paul looked from the mother and baby to the husband, who obviously didn't care much for the child his wife had just delivered. He nodded and followed the weathered farmer into the main part of the house. His own neighbor, Ronald Ulster, stood by the unlit hearth, twisting his hat in his hands.

"Mr. Ulster," Paul said in greeting, reaching out a hand.

"Paul," the man said, shaking his hand. "I'm sorry to be the one to tell you, but your father has passed. Happened about two hours ago. Me and the missus stopped by to see if you folks needed anything. He was … he was in a bad way. Said you was here. We stayed with him and did all we could, but it wasn't enough. I'm mighty sorry."

Paul released the man's hand and let his own fall to his side. His head seemed suddenly very heavy. "Thank you," he murmured.

"Hell of a night to die," Mr. Ulster said. "I wouldn't want to die on this night."

Paul looked up. "That's … " he stopped. "Excuse me."

He rushed back behind the curtain and snatched the infant from Mrs. Groves. He brought it near the lamp. The baby did not cry. Paul looked into the knowing brown eyes. The child grinned at him, then winked.

The baby was shaking. No, Paul realized, his own hands were trembling.

"See what you did," Mrs. Bennett said. "You provided the shell for something that ain't supposed to be in this world no more."

"Father," Paul whispered.

# ABOUT THE AUTHOR

Steven E. Wedel lives in central Oklahoma with his dogs Bear and Sweet Pea, and Cleo the cat. He began writing in the mid-1980s and has kept at it despite numerous disappointments and setbacks. Steve has a bachelor's degree in journalism from the University of Central Oklahoma and a master's degree in liberal studies from the University of Oklahoma. He has worked as a machinist, bookseller, stock clerk, journalist, public relations specialist and is now an English teacher most of the year.

Visit him online at www.stevenewedel.com.